ORVILLE'S ODYSSEY

ODYSSEY

CHRIS L. DEMAREST

Prentice-Hall Books for Young Readers
A Division of Simon & Schuster, Inc.
New York

For
Christopher
and
Jeffrey

PRENTICE-HALL BOOKS FOR YOUNG READERS is a trademark of Simon & Schuster, Inc.

Manufactured in Spain

10 9 8 7 6 5 4 3 2 1

Library of Congress Cataloging in Publication Data

Demarest, Chris L.
   Orville's Odyssey.

Summary: Orville's fishing expedition becomes a strange adventure when a large fish pulls him into a puddle and he struggles to escape. (1. Fishing—Fiction. 2. Stories without words) I. Title.
PZ7.D39140r 1986 (E) 86-8439
ISBN: 0-13-642851-7